#know your worth

Written with love by
Stephanie Solomon

Give life a meaning!

ISBN: 978-1-54394-440-2

It's like having nothing;
it can't even pay the rent.

When Penelope heard this, her face and heart became so sad.

Her friends called her Penny;
now she thought that was bad.

Every time she heard her nickname,
she doubted herself and goals to fame.

How could she become anything if she felt worthless and ashamed?

She went for a walk outside and
noticed a Penny on the ground.

She smiled.

To her surprise, it was good luck she found.

Great things started happening after her lucky find.
Her heart grew even more happy and kind.

She stopped doubting herself,
making more goals and dreams.

She made short goals and long goals
anything she could, or so it seems...

On her adventures and just daily walks,
she'd stumble across a random Penny.

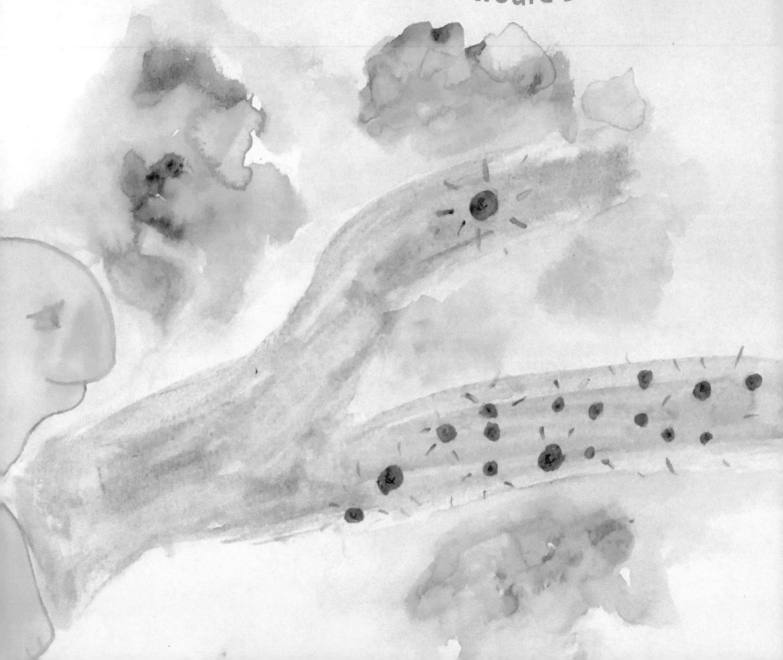

Some days it would be one,
and some days it would be many.

It was a reminder that every time she found one, to never give up.

To avoid seeing life half empty and always a full cup.

Be positive
when things don't go right.
Focus on the good and not lose sight.

Be gracious and thankful. Be humble and helpful.

Remind yourself that other people's words shouldn't affect your greatness, or life for long.

Be kind, be strong & funny when you can.

You are worthy, enough and the world's greatest fan.

ILLUSTRATED BY:

Molly Harris